# Emoji Adventures #4

# Reality TV

ISBN 978-0692666494

## #MomTime

"This is SO UNFAIR!!!" Kevin shouts.

For once, I agree with my brother.

"Don't you understand what you're doing?!"

"We have to put a stop to this," Kevin adds.

But it's no use. Mom's got the TV in the family room tonight and there are no ifs, ands, or buts about it.

"You two get the TV 24/7," Mom says as we try to escort her out of the room. "And you'd take it 25/7 if you could. Tonight's my turn; there's absolutely nothing unfair about it."

"But *Mom...*" I start to say.

She shakes her head. "*Real Housewives of Emojiville* starts in twenty minutes and my girlfriends are on their way over. If you care so much about watching TV, you can join us."

Kevin and I *could* watch videos on our phones but tonight we wanted to watch a movie on the big screen.    When the doorbell rings, I know we've lost the fight.

One by one, Mom's friends show up. First is Nancy, who's really nice but is too touchy for my taste. Immediately she pulls me into a big hug.

"Annie!" she finally lets go of me only to pinch my cheeks. "I can't believe how much you've grown since the last time I saw you!"

"Me neither."  I don't remind her I ran into her at the mall last week.

Next is Rita. She's a free spirit and the only grown-up in Emojiville who's usually eager to help Kevin with his pranks. She even got him fireworks for the Fourth of July last year. I always like seeing Rita, but I'm careful to stay on her good side.

"Let the festivities begin!" Rita shouts. "I brought enough  popcorn to feed all of Emojiville!"

Last to arrive is Sharon, Mom's grumpiest friend. I swear I haven't seen Sharon crack a smile *ever*. I can't figure out why the others like spending time with her - or vice versa, considering she's always complaining about something and never seems to be having any fun.

"Parking was a nightmare," Sharon says. "To think I went through all of that just to watch a TV show."

"I'm not going to listen to Sharon complain all night," Kevin whispers as he leaves the room. His robot, SAM, follows close behind.

I decide to stay and watch the show. It's actually kind of cool hanging out with Mom and her friends. Half the fun is watching the women's reactions to the show, arguing and fighting about the people on the screen.

"You are *way* more entertaining than the housewives on TV," I tell them.

Dad comes running in from the kitchen, a half-eaten piece of chicken in his hand.

"That's brilliant!" he shouts. "You women *should* have your *own* show! I'll be your producer. Annie's right, you're better than this cast!"

Rita immediately cracks up. "Count me in. Sounds like a blast!"

Mom, who's already blushing, blushes even more. "You think people would watch *us*?"

"You four are hilarious," Dad says.

Nancy pulls the others into a hug.

"But it won't work without all four of you," Dad says.

All eyes are on Sharon.

"Oh, brother. Fine," Sharon moans. "I'll do it if it means Nancy will let go of me."

Dad holds up his drumstick as if it were a glass then makes a toast. Is Mom headed to primetime?

#BehindTheScenes

 Dad and the ladies get right to work making test videos. Everyone gets really into it, even Sharon, who still won't crack a smile but gets annoyed when the camera isn't around to film her best moments.

"I just did something funny," Sharon says. "Did you record it?"

"I missed it," Dad says. "Do it again."

"You call yourself a producer?" she complains.

Kevin and I are in a few scenes with Mom and I can tell she's having the time of her life. I've never seen her look so proud (which is saying something, because Mom *always* looks proud).

It's not long before the women start thinking of themselves as full-fledged stars. Mom gets a haircut with highlights, a manicure, and a whole new wardrobe. And the show hasn't even been picked up yet.

Finally Dad has his big meeting with E!moji TV, the network that produces *Real Housewives of Emojiville*. All day long we're on pins and needles waiting to hear if Mom and her friends will get their big break.

Dad gets home just as Mom is serving dinner. He hands her a bouquet of flowers.

"Does this mean...?" Mom asks, nearly dropping the pot of spaghetti.

"I have good news and bad news." Dad dramatically takes a seat at the table. "I'll start with the bad news."

Uh-oh.

"The network passed on our version of *Real Housewives of Emojiville*."

Mom freezes for a moment though she doesn't lose the cheerful smile on her face. (I knew I got that positive gene from somewhere.) Still, I can tell she's upset because she dishes pasta onto her plate with great intensity.

"My friends will be so disappointed," Mom finally says.

"It's a disappointment for *all* of us," Dad says. "I'm sorry, honey. I don't know why they didn't go for it."

"I'm sorry to disappoint you kids," Mom says. "I know you loved filming the scenes where I drove you to school and practice."

I think she wants *us* to be upset so we don't have to focus on *her* being upset.

"Well," Dad says. "That's where there's good news. The network loved the footage with Annie and Kevin and they want to make a reality show about them."

What?! I can't believe it. Me, as the star of a reality show?! I was fine to make cameos in Mom's.

Mom stares at her plate of spaghetti in a daze.

Dad continues. "They loved how different Annie and Kevin are from one another, especially as twins. I told them because you're both trained actors, you'll surely be up to the job. And we can use SAM's internal recording device to help get footage around the clock."

"But we're *not* trained actors," I say.

Dad ignores me.

"They're even going to give Kevin a pranking budget. How funny is that?"

"I'M IN!" Kevin says excitedly.

"Mom," I say, "We don't have to do the show if it will upset you and your friends. I know you were looking forward to it."

Mom speaks up, finally taking a break from staring at her pasta. "Sure, it would've been fun to have our own reality show, but you're my kids and opportunity's knocking."

I guess that means I have to answer the door.

## #CameraReady

 Within two weeks, *Real Siblings of Emojiville* begins filming. I try to keep it under wraps so my life can stay as normal as possible, but it's not easy to keep it a secret when cameras follow you everywhere you go. Pretty soon a lot of people know about the pilot and they want in on the action.

"ANNIE!!!" Tiffany calls when she sees me at my lockers with the camera crew. She pulls me into a hug. "How's my best friend today?"

"I'm... good?" I say, confused to see Tiffany being so friendly. "Had to think there for a sec."

Laughter rings out behind me so loudly that I jump. It's Zoe.

"'Had to think about it!'" she says through a fit of laughter. "That's a good one!"

Zoe moves in close enough to ensure she gets on camera. She's always laughing at Tiffany's jokes, but it's the first time she's ever responded to me that way.

"Are we still hanging out tonight?" Tiffany asks me.

"Tonight? Did we have plans?"

"OMG, how did you forget?" Tiffany asks.

"Probably because *we* had plans," Zoe interrupts.

I, of course, have no plans with either of them.

"Actually," a low voice chimes in, "I believe Annie has plans with *me.*"

I turn to face Austin, Mr. Cool. Now I really know something's up because Austin normally doesn't want anything to do with me.

I figure they must want my attention so they can be on the reality show too. I wish it had more to do with who I am as a person, but I try to look on the bright side - at least now I'm *somewhat* popular.

"Sorry, but I already have plans tonight." I don't mention that plans are just my homework. "But maybe this weekend?"

"DEFINITELY," Zoe and Austin say in unison.

"Text me later, okay?" Tiffany hugs me and leaves with her entourage.

Dot and Kevin are also acting a little differently now that the cameras are on. Even though we're each other's best friends, having the cameras around makes it hard for us to have normal conversations.

"I have a secret to tell you," Billy says, before he looks at the camera crew. "Oh, wait. Never mind."

"Psst!" says the cameraman. "Say it! The viewers will eat it up!"

But I can tell Billy doesn't want to confide anything secret on national television.

"Um... my secret is that... I really like pizza," he says.

"OMG, Billy, as if we didn't already know that." Dot doesn't realize he's kidding.

The cameraman shakes his head in disappointment.

When I get home, Dad's in the living room with the new producer. Even though I always try to see the best in people, there's something about this guy I immediately don't like, starting with the fact that he doesn't call me Annie and instead refers to me as 'the girl.'

"This must be the girl," he says when I walk in. "I'm Ari Emoticon, your producer. You might recognize my work on *The Real Garbage Men of Emojiville* or *Pigs in Pants*."

"Oh yeah," I say, pretending to be familiar with his shows.

"Ari has big plans for you," Dad says. "Including some changes we made to your room today."

They changed my room without asking? I run down the hall to see what they've done. When I open my door, I gasp: they've redone *everything*. All my old stuff is gone, from my horse posters to my trophies. In their place, Ari put in a ball pit, a wall size TV screen, multiple size tablets, bean bag chairs, and even a tire swing.

I'm not sure how I feel about all the changes to my room until I notice a new bookcase that's covered from floor to ceiling with horse figurines and books.

"OMG – the entire collection of Palomino Ponies!"

Suddenly I think this might turn out okay after all.

## #LongDivision

 Now that Ari Emoticon is involved in the reality show, the filming schedule is even more intense. When we started, the camera crews were around fifty percent of the time, but now it's closer to ninety percent. They film me flossing, eating, getting ready for school... You name it, they film it, *especially* if it's unflattering. One time, they caught me yawning in front of the TV.

"That's great!" the producer says. "We can edit that shot into a classroom scene."

The first big day of filming this week is at the annual math decathlon held at the Emojiville High auditorium. I've been a Mathlete since first grade and the decathlon is a great opportunity to show off my skills (or fail miserably in front of the cameras and crowd.) It's always nerve-wracking and this year is no exception. In fact, if anything, this time around will be even more intimidating because the whole thing could be broadcast on E!moji TV.

I'm shocked to see the large crowd filling the auditorium. Usually it's just parents that show up to watch the decathlon. But this year, everyone in town wants to be a part of *Real Siblings of Emojiville*. (Why else would Tiffany, Zoe, and Austin come watch a group of math nerds do long division?)

I was worried Ms. Zimmerman wouldn't want the crew to interfere with the decathlon, but instead she's thrilled with the publicity.

 "This is a great opportunity for you to be a role model. A reality star *and* a good student," she tells me.

"Do you think Mr. Emoticon would listen to my pitch for *Real Mathematicians of Emojiville*?"

As soon as the competition gets started though, things start to go downhill. My first question is a no brainer: what's twenty divided by four?

"Five," I say confidently.

"Cut!" Ari yells from the crowd. "Annie, you need to create suspense. Act like you don't know the answer right away."

"Suspense?" Ms. Zimmerman asks. "It's a competition, not a mystery! Besides, this isn't a film set!"

"Looks like one to me." Ari motions to the cameras and crew around the auditorium. "Take two! Action!"

"What's twenty divided by four?" Ms. Zimmerman asks again with flair, showing off for the director.

I pretend to think about it for a while before finally shouting, "FIVE!!!"

An illuminated sign above the stage flashes 'APPLAUSE' and the whole audience claps enthusiastically as though I just solved the world's most difficult math formula.

"Go, Annie, go!" Dot and Billy shout, louder than everyone else.

"Look at those two cheering their heads off," Ari says to the cameraman. "Get a close-up."

The rest of the competition is equally embarrassing, although I smile through it. At one point, a nervous student named Claire is in the middle of answering a particularly tough division question.

"Sorry," Claire says. "I just want to check my work one more time."

"Will someone get this girl off the stage?" Ari yells. "We don't have all day."

I can tell Ms. Zimmerman is upset, but she's hiding it as best as she can to stay on the producer's' good side. But the reality is, she spent months planning this event and it's being taken over by a pushy Hollywood executive.

After forty-five minutes of interruptions, Ari and his crew leave the auditorium.

"That's a wrap, people!" Ari calls.

"Next stop, the water park to film Kevin!"

The whole crew leaves. So does most of the crowd, eagerly following them to the park.

So much for being a role model.

#RealityBites

 When I get home from the decathlon, the house is empty with no cameras in sight. Claire ended up winning the decathlon, which made me happy after the repeated interruptions. Still, I could tell everyone was a little irritated with me for bringing along the whole crew. I try to focus on the excitement of my new life, but a part of me misses the way things were before all the cameras showed up.

Freckles follows me to my room, where I plan taking a well-deserved nap.

 Working on the decathlon and the reality show at the same time has been exhausting.

On my way upstairs, I get a whiff of something terrible. What is Kevin up to now?

When I open my bedroom door, I'm greeted by a room full of pigs.

"AHH!!!"

*That's* where the smell is

coming from.

Freckles sprints back down the stairs, wanting nothing to do with this.

"Cut!" Ari shouts, popping out of the closet.

Kevin is with him, laughing hysterically. SAM does his programmed robotic laugh. "HA, HA, HA."

Was this Kevin's idea or did Ari make him do it?  Kevin's expanded prank budget is now my nightmare come to life.

"Let's go again," Ari says. "But next time you need to scream Kevin's name instead of just saying 'Ahh'. The facial expression was great - really horrifying - but we want it to be clear that Kevin did it. Let's get Freckles back in here for Take Two."

I almost never lose my cool but can't help myself. "This is ridiculous! All this filming is ruining my life!"

"Keep the cameras rolling," Ari instructs the crew. "She's going to have a meltdown. This is gold."

"I never knew what a studio budget would do for my pranking," Kevin says gleefully. "This is the best thing that's ever happened to me."

Suddenly Mom pops her head in, wearing a new dress and more makeup than she's ever worn in her life.

"What's all the commotion?" she says into the camera.

"They filled my room with pigs!"

Mom cracks up. "That's hysterical! Bravo, Kevin."

"I know I won't get anywhere arguing, Mom wishes this were *her* show. She obviously doesn't want to hear me complaining about being the star.

"DAD!" I call. "I need to talk to you!"

Dad approaches with two cell phones, one up to each ear. He shakes his head to tell me he can't talk.

"Tell their agents we have no time to meet with them until after Friday," he says into one phone. "Tell them I'm around every day this week - Friday is totally fine," he says into the other.

"Dad!" I say. "I need to talk to you!"

"He's in two very important meetings right now," Mom says. "Honey, I know this show is a big commitment, but think of the opportunity you're getting! Not everyone gets the chance to be the star of a TV series. Enjoy it because other people - like me! - wish they were in your shoes."

I remember how excited Mom was a few weeks ago, so I don't argue. She's right; It's up to me to face even the pigs with a smile.

# #Revamp

One week later, the show premieres on E!moji TV. The network gives it a huge build-up. There are commercials for it every half hour and a giant billboard downtown that has a shot of me looking horrified while Kevin laughs. It debuts right after *Real Housewives of Emojiville*. After my pep talk with Mom, I'm excited to see myself on TV.

The first episode is, in my opinion, a huge success. The clips from the decathlon make me look smart. They even changed the footage to make it appear that I won. And I hate to admit it, but the clips of Kevin's pranks are hilarious. Everyone cracks up as we watch his crazy schemes, from a flash mob in the school cafeteria to changing the school bell to a cuckoo clock. Even the pig scene makes me laugh. (Although the smell probably won't leave my room for months)

Kevin, Dad, and I are all happy with the pilot episode. Mom looks less happy because her scenes got cut but still says she's proud of her children.

The one person who isn't happy with the pilot is Ari Emoticon who calls the family into an urgent meeting at his office.

"The ratings were less than impressive." Ari's doing pushups on the floor of his office overlooking the city. "Turns out your lives are a little too normal for viewers. Because of that, we're giving you new back stories."

What?!

"Annie, you're the former Little Miss Emojiville," he says. "You were crowned at six years-old and it was the best day of your life. Now you're trying to make sense of things after that epic victory."

"But -" I start.

"And Kevin," he continues, "your new back story is that you weren't always so devilish. You became a prankster after eating a poisonous piece of seafood two years ago that changed your brain chemistry. At some point we'll need you to tearfully remember that moment on camera."

Finally, something to explain why Kevin acts the way he does, although it does seem a bit far-fetched.

"One more thing," Ari says. "We didn't get good ratings on your BFFs, so we're giving you a new best friend. Allow me to introduce you to Hank, your new costar."

Suddenly, a boy my age walks into the room. He has thick glasses and huge teeth. I recognize him from Dad's emoji meter. Biggest nerd ever.

 "Greetings, my fellow earthling," he says.

My heart sinks. Is this guy really going to be my new BFF?

# #NoNewFriends

 That evening, I invite Billy and Dot over to tell them the news. We go to the backyard where, thankfully, the cameraman has taken a break because his car got towed. (Looks like Kevin's taking pranking into his own hands.) Billy and Dot are both horrified to hear they've been replaced.

"They didn't give us any warning!" Billy cries. "I had so many big plans!"

"We can still fight our way in," says Dot with determination. "Since we're your real best friends, we'll still be around all the time. All we need to do is figure out how to appeal to the audience."

She gets to work thinking of ways to raise her game on the show.

"I've got it!" she announces after a few minutes. "I need to make a cool entrance."

"What about me?" Billy asks.

"Sorry - It's every emoji for themselves."

I guess desperate times call for desperate measures.

When Hank arrives, I try to make conversation but he's very shy.

"You just moved here?" I ask, smiling brightly.

"Um... yeah," Hank answers.

If Ari thought my real friends were boring, why'd he replace them with this guy?

"Because you're the former Miss Emojiville, I thought you'd be the perfect person to show me the town," Hank says.

He certainly doesn't sound very excited.

"That's right," I say. "I'm definitely the former Miss Emojiville. It was the happiest day of my life." This back story is ridiculous.

I introduce Hank to Billy. Hank is still awkward and seems a little weirded out to be talking to a kid made of poop.

"Where's Dot?" I can't wait for this to be over. "She said she'd be here."

Suddenly Dot slides out from behind a tree, flying through the air in a karate pose.

"Dot's on duty!" she declares in a voice that doesn't sound anything like how she usually talks.

"Huh?" I ask.

"Dot's on duty!" she repeats, directly into the camera

This is not good.

For the rest of the week, the four of us try to hang out but the dynamic is weird. I'm forced to pretend I'm a former beauty queen, Dot keeps shouting her catchphrase at inappropriate moments, Hank is impossible to hold a conversation with, and Billy keeps getting pushed out of the shot. I try to stay optimistic about the whole thing; at least I have friends, right?

The next day though, everything changes. The four of us meet up at my lockers with the camera crew but this time it's Billy who shows up late. When he finally appears, he looks distraught.

"Look what I got in the mail yesterday," he says.

He holds up a handwritten note:

*GET THAT PIECE OF POOP OFF THE SHOW!*

"Oh, Billy," I say. "That's so mean."

"The viewing public has spoken."

Billy hangs his head.

"It's gonna be okay," I say. "Right, guys?"

"Uh, sure," Hank says.

"Dot's on duty!" Dot shouts to  the camera.

This might be a reality show, but it's far from reality right now.

## #MeetUp

 That Saturday, the producers arrange for Hank and me to go to the arcade. I ask to bring Billy and Dot along but the producers won't allow it. I really don't want to spend the whole day with Hank, but Dad reminds me we have an obligation to the show. Besides, I don't want to hurt Hank's feelings.

I arrive before Hank and wait at the pinball machine, hoping maybe he'll be more talkative one-on-one. I wait for almost half an hour as the camera films me playing different games. I'm about to head home when Hank appears, trailed by another camera crew.

"Hi, Hank." I smile even though I wish I'd just been able to go home.

"Well, if it isn't the famed Miss Emojiville. Always a pleasure," Hank says.

Huh?! Two days ago he could barely say hello. Now leans over like he's going to give me a hug but at the last minute extends his hand for me to shake.

"You come here often?" he asks.

"The arcade?" I ask. "Sometimes."

"Sometimes! You are spicy," Hank laughs.

"Sorry, what did you just say?" I ask. "It sounded like you just called me spicy."

Is this the same Hank that hasn't been able to string two words together all week?

"Let's play some pinball," Hank suggests. "Don't worry - I'll go easy on you."

I start to ask him a question but he's already on the other side of arcade.

"Watch an old pro at work." Hank stares at the machine as if he's trying to figure out how it works.

It's strange - even though Hank's being more talkative, he still seems uncomfortable, which makes *me* feel uncomfortable. Still, I try to smile and laugh along. I don't really get his jokes, but at least he's trying.

"After this, I'd like to take you out to a nice Italian shuttle," he says as we play air hockey. "Er, I mean, a nice Italian supper."

What is with this guy?

"Sounds fun, but maybe we can do something a little more low-key." I know how hard it can be to make friends so I give Hank the benefit of the doubt, even

though I'm starting to wonder if he wants

to be more than friends.

"You must be talking to the wrong

guy. Hank doesn't do low-key," he

responds. "Nuh-uh, he doesn't."

"I think I should go meet up with

Billy and Dot." I feel a little guilty for how

badly I want this outing to be over. "They like to be low-key too."

"Well, hater's gonna..." He pauses with a confused look on his face. "Huh?" he asks, which is exactly what I want to say. "I can't hear you," he finally says.

"I didn't say anything." WHAT IS GOING ON?

To make the day even worse, Kevin appears.

"How's your date going?" he asks with a smirk.

"It's not a date!" I say.

"Isn't it? Nudge her." Hank looks confused for a moment. "Oh, whoops." He nudges me with his elbow.

"Ow!"

"It's a date... with destiny!" Kevin suddenly reveals a water balloon.

I duck but just before Kevin throws the water balloon, Ari Emoticon runs in and shields me.

"That's not in the script!" Ari gets nailed with the balloon.

I'm relieved Ari came to my defense but he's so angry it's also kind of scary.

"You're not authorized to be on this set!" Ari yells. "You only prank when I tell you to prank."

"I can't help it!" Kevin responds. "Don't you remember the poisonous fish that made me crazy?"

But Ari is not amused. "Kevin, we had a plan for this scene. It's Hank and Annie's first date."

"It's not a date!" I say.

"Isn't it?" Hank says again.

Suddenly something occurs to me.

"Wait a minute!" I turn to Hank. "Is someone feeding you lines?"

"No way!" Hank's face is flushed. "Okay, fine, yes."

Hank pulls an earpiece out of his ear. I can faintly hear someone's voice shouting, "Why'd you tell her?!"

OMG. Of *course* the producers were behind this. It finally makes sense. I knew Hank seemed different today.

"The whole scene is ruined," Ari says angrily.

"This show is cramping my style," Kevin says.

"Mine too," I say.

We turn to Hank, who shrugs; he has nothing to say now that no one's feeding him lines.

#WitsEnd

 That evening all I want to do is talk to Mom and Dad about my frustration with the show. I gave it a try but after these last few weeks, I'm ready to be away from the cameras for a while.

When I get home from the shoot, Mom greets me at the front door. She's wearing tons of makeup and another new outfit, so I know the camera crew must be inside.

Hey, I know - I'll start talking about wanting the cameras to go away... while on camera.

"Mom, we need to talk." I join her in the living room. "All this filming is making it hard for me to be my upbeat, happy self. The producers keep putting me in these crazy situations and I feel like I don't have control over anything anymore."

Mom's about to interrupt- probably to tell me how much she wishes it were *her* show - when Kevin appears in a huff.

"This show has to end!" he insists. "No one tells me when I can or can't prank. That's like telling a fish when it can swim!"

Normally I'd never take Kevin's side, but on this particular issue I do. I'm glad he's also asking for the cameras to go away.

"I guess I see why you two are so overwhelmed," Mom says. Of course she hears me now that Kevin's unhappy. "This is something I guess you'll have to take up with -"

"KIDS!!!" Dad yells from outside.

We hear a few honks and look through the open front door to the street. Dad is parking a brand new golf cart in the driveway. Beside him is his new assistant, Martin, who looks stressed out.

"Check out my new ride, kids!" Dad calls cheerfully. "And before you ask, no, you're not allowed to drive it. Martin, where are you?"

"Here, sir," Martin says.

"Run to the coffee shop and grab me a decaf soy vanilla-caramel hybrid latte with foam. And make sure it's not lukewarm this time."

"Okay, Mr. Emoji," Martin says. "Anything else?"

"Pick up my dry cleaning," Dad replies. "Then get me on the phone with the execs over at Bravomoji."

"But sir, it's 5PM on a Saturday..." Martin begins.

"I don't want to hear excuses," Dad says. "I want to see results."

"Yes, sir." Martin scurries off to run his errands.

67

"Great news, kids!" Dad says as he approaches the house. "You're booked to 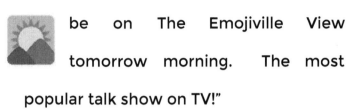 be on The Emojiville View tomorrow morning. The most popular talk show on TV!"

"Tomorrow morning?!"

"We're planning a *live* episode of *Real Siblings* at the end of next week! You're going on The Emojiville View to promote it."

"Dad," I say, "this show is taking over our lives. That's what we were talking to Mom about when you got here."

"Nonsense!" Dad says. "You two are stars! Don't give up the limelight when you have it."

With that, he picks up his phone. "Martin, I'd like to change my coffee order." He then puts his hand over the phone and turns to us.

"You're on a national talk show tomorrow - start preparing!"

# #TheEmojivilleView

Kevin and I are up before sunrise the next morning to be on *The Emojiville View*. They've also asked Billy, Dot, Hank, and SAM to join us for the interview, so we all meet outside the studio where paparazzi lined up to take our pictures. I run inside to hair and makeup to avoid the cameras; everyone else ambles in slowly, enjoying the moment.

Dot and Billy are especially excited. Dot keeps rehearsing her entrance, each time making it crazier than the time before.

"Dot's on duty!" she shouts, almost knocking over a chair when she slides into the room.

"Tip of the tongue, tip of the teeth, tip of the tongue, tip of the teeth." Billy's in the corner, practicing voice warm-ups.

Even I'm a little excited by the hubbub. It's hard not to feel good about yourself when everyone is telling you you're a star.

Finally it's showtime. Kevin and I go out first. We enter the set to thunderous applause and join the hosts: Linda, Maureen, and Janice.

The hosts couldn't be sweeter, singing our praises in front of the audience.

"These are Emojiville's favorite kids," Linda declares. "Annie, young girls all over Emojiville are looking at you and saying, 'I want to be that good at math!'"

I'm not sure that's true, but it would sure make me happy if it is.

Linda continues. "And Kevin, you're giving a lot of pranksters some pretty good ideas..."

The audience bursts into applause. Maybe being a reality star isn't so bad after all. When else am I going to get this kind of attention?

"So tell us about your upcoming telecast," Maureen says.

"It's going to be the realest reality TV show ever." I practiced this part of the interview dozens of times. "A totally live episode of *Real Siblings*."

"Think Kevin has any tricks up his sleeve?" Janice asks.

Kevin just grins and rubs his hands together.

"Think so? I *know* so! He wouldn't my twin if he wasn't planning something." My response brings more applause from the audience.

Later, they bring out the rest of the cast. Dot makes a grand entrance shouting her catchphrase over and over again. Hank, meanwhile, looks like he'd rather be anywhere else.

"So, Hank, will you tell us about your relationship with Annie?" Linda asks. "It seems like you two have a *very* close connection."

I keep smiling but want to curl up under the couch and die.

"Um, well, uh, yes Linda, it's a great connection." Hank pulls out a rose from his jacket and hands it to me. "We're in love."

The audience claps so loudly, no one hears me say it's not true.

"That is so beautiful," Janice says. "Ahh, young love."

Just as I'm about to respond, Janice introduces Billy who's met with boos from the audience.

Linda tries to calm the crowd.

"Now, Billy," Linda says. "Many of our viewers think you're too dirty for TV. They don't like your potty humor."

"They don't know me well enough to judge," Billy says.

"He's a great person," I say. "One of my best friends."

Linda calms the booing crowd once more and Billy runs off stage.

When we leave the studio, there's a mob of protesters waiting outside. Many of them carry signs: *GET THIS FILTH OFF*

*TV!* Next to the message is a picture of Billy with a red "X" over his face.

OMG!

"Stop that!" I shout.

"Leave our friend alone!" Dot cries.

Billy quickly runs away. We're about to follow him when two girls approach us for our autographs.

"Annie, you're my hero!" one of the girls says.

"Dot's on duty!" the other shouts.

It's hard to say no to two girls this sweet. Before we know it, there's a line of fans waiting for autographs and paparazzi everywhere. By the time we're done, Billy is nowhere to be found.

# #Controversy

The next day is Monday and everyone at school has seen us on the talk show. Tiffany is relentless about getting on.

"You looked *amazing*," she gushes. "I can't wait to see the live episode. By the way, if you need a replacement for Billy, I could probably clear some time in my busy schedule to give you a hand."

"I think we're all set," I say. "But thanks for the offer."

Dot is also swarmed with fans who call out her catchphrase when she passes by. It's pretty fun walking through the halls with her - for once, we're the most popular kids in school.

Hank is waiting at my locker with a  bouquet of flowers.

"How are you, sweetheart?" He hands me the flowers and tries to kiss me.

"Hank, for the last time, I'm not your girlfriend!" I push him away. "If you want to be friends, we can. But that's all we'll ever be."

"If you say so." He turns to the camera and winks.

Hank gestures to the white bud sticking out of his ear - an earpiece again. I wish they weren't still feeding him lines, but I'm glad he at least told me this time.

We wait at my locker for Billy but he never shows up.

"I hope this doesn't have anything to do with the protesters yesterday," I whisper to Dot.

After school, we hop on our bikes and race over to Billy's house, ditching the camera crew in the process. Hank joins us even though

I'm starting to wish he would leave me alone.

We fight through crowds of protesters to reach the front door. Billy answers, looking exhausted.

"The protesters followed me home from the talk show," Billy says.

"That's horrible!"

"It's so unfair!" Dot agrees.

"It gets worse," Billy says. "I'm banned from school because of the outcry. The school says they can't take the risk of having me on campus. I have to be homeschooled until the controversy dies down."

Everyone at school *loves* Billy, even on his toxic days.

Suddenly my frustration about the show comes back full force. Being a celebrity is fun, but it's nothing compared to having your best friends by your side.

"This show is messing up our lives," I say.

"I hope this all blows over soon," Billy agrees.

"It will." I try to be positive, although I'm getting worried.

How can we put an end  to this mess?

# #HatchingAPlan

Leaving Billy's house, I'm worried we'll run into the camera crew, but it looks like we lost them. Dot has to visit her aunt, so Hank and I walk back alone. I use the opportunity to talk.

"I know it's hard to make friends." I smile as sweetly as I can to lighten the blow. "But I need a little space."

"I'm sorry I keep bugging you," he says. "But there's something I want to discuss."

"Are the producers putting you up to this?" I ask.

"I promise they aren't." He pulls the earpiece out and clicks it off. "In fact, I want to talk to you about the show. Hearing you and Billy got me thinking about how much I hate this show too. I never should've said I'd do it."

"You're miserable too?"

"I don't know why you're surprised," he says. "Look at me! I'm not an actor. I'm a nerd! I don't want a girlfriend - I'm ten!"

"So why'd you take the job?" I ask.

"My parents thought it would help

me come out of my shell," Hank says.

"But the producer is having me do things

that aren't 'me' at all. It's making it even harder for me to be who I really am."

"That does it," I say. "We need to end this series once and for all. My parents aren't any help. They want this show to keep going. We need to do it on our own."

I know Mom and Dad are going to be upset, but I don't care now that I know the whole cast is as miserable as I am.

"But how do we stop it?" Hank asks. "You and I aren't the kind of people who can ruin a huge production."

"I know someone who can," I say.

"Kevin," we say in unison.

As we high five, I can't help but notice how much less awkward Hank is now that the pressure is off. Maybe we'll stay friends after this.

"I'll talk to Kevin right away," I say. "But we don't have much time."

"What do you mean?" Hank asks.

"We have two days to plan. Because we're going to wreck the show on live TV."

# #TheBigDay

The next few days are a blur. Between rehearsals for the live episode with the producers and planning our secret sabotage with Kevin and Hank, I barely have time to sleep.

I should be exhausted by the time the big shoot rolls around, but I'm so nervous, I have a rush of adrenaline instead.

Everybody else seems nervous too: Ari paces around the house yelling at the crew, Mom changes outfits a million times, and Dad has so many phone calls going that even Martin has to hold up a phone for him to talk into. To make things even *more* stressful, the head of the studio, Donna Bigwig, is here.

Nancy, Rita, and Sharon all arrive in outfits as elaborate as Mom's. I bet it took Dad twenty phone calls to get Mom and her friends invited into this live episode.

"Ladies, we made it!" Nancy says delightedly.

"I hope everyone's ready to have  a blast!" Rita cheers.

"This was a terrible idea," Sharon gripes. "We're all going to look terrible and everyone in town will judge us. It's a no-win situation."

"Everyone is going to judge *you* for being such a spoil-sport," Rita quips.

"We're low on mics!" one of the producers calls as they get everyone prepared for the shoot.

"The kids already have theirs," Mom says. "Hey, where are the kids anyway?"

The grownups have been so distracted, they haven't noticed Kevin and I aren't there.

In Dad's editing room, Kevin and I go over the plan. We put our heads together to stand up for what's right, and that puts a smile on my face for real this time.

"WE'RE READY TO SHOOT!!!" Ari barks.

"So are we," I answer.

You want reality? You've got it.

## #LightsCameraAction

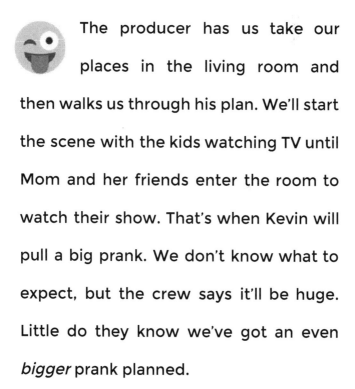 The producer has us take our places in the living room and then walks us through his plan. We'll start the scene with the kids watching TV until Mom and her friends enter the room to watch their show. That's when Kevin will pull a big prank. We don't know what to expect, but the crew says it'll be huge. Little do they know we've got an even *bigger* prank planned.

"Okay, people, quiet on the set," Ari says. "Lights... Camera... Action!"

"What a boring day!" I say.

"I wish there was something fun to do," Hank says.

"Let's watch our own show!" Dot adds.

 I can't believe how boring the dialogue is. I can't WAIT to be off this series.

"That's a great idea!" Kevin says.

"Affirmative," SAM agrees.

Billy says nothing - the producers haven't fired him but told him not to talk.

Kevin picks up the remote and my heart starts pounding. *This is it*, I think. The moment of truth.

What comes on the screen *isn't* our regular show but the footage from SAM's internal video camera that he's filmed over the past few weeks. In the footage, Ari's standing in the kitchen with Kevin. I can tell everyone in the room is startled - *this* isn't supposed to be on TV!

"Kevin, we've got to raise the stakes of the show," Ari says onscreen. "It can't just be fun and games. We need *drama*. That's why we think you should kill the cat."

My mom and her friends gasp. Wait

till they get a load of the rest!

"I'll never kill Freckles!" Kevin

says in the video. "Annie loves that

cat!"

"If ratings don't pick up, you won't

have a choice," Ari answers.

Dad turns to Ari and asks him to

explain.

But Dad's interrupted when the

footage cuts to a shot of Ari on the

phone, pacing around our backyard.

"We'll make sure a bike

comes in front of the mom's

car, forcing her to stop. Then

we'll have a garbage truck rear-end her, dumping trash all over her car."

"What did you just say?" No  pleasant face on Mom now.

"What is this?!" Ari screams at the TV. "This isn't part of the show!"

The footage cuts to Ari in Dad's office with a big poster board and a marker. *GET THIS FILTH OFF TV!* he writes in big letters.

"I knew there was something fishy about the protests," Billy says. "Those protesters were hired. Ari made the signs himself!"

"This is fake!" Ari screams. "I don't know where you got this footage but none of it is real! This is a setup!"

"This footage comes from SAM's hidden camera," Kevin says proudly.

Ari is about to start screaming when Donna Bigwig, the head of E!Moji TV, stands up.

"In all my years of producing television, I have never seen such outrageous behavior! This is absolutely reprehensible. You are fired, Ari. Do you hear me? FIRED!"

Ari knocks over the camera equipment until people from the crew restrain him and take him outside.

Dad, who's never been one to miss an opportunity, speaks up. "Well, I guess the show needs a new producer," he tells Ms. Bigwig. "And as their manager and agent, I'm just the man for the job."

To my relief, Ms. Bigwig shakes her head. "This show is over," she says.

"I'm pulling the plug right now."

# #BackToRealLife

"This is so unfair!"

Kevin and I beg Mom to give up the TV room, where she's hosting her weekly viewing party of *Emojiville's Next Top Model.*

"Remember what happened *last* time we went through this?" I ask.

"Sorry kids, the girls are already on their way," Mom says.

"Well, my friends are *also* on their way," I argue.

"If they want to join us, they can," Mom says. "It wouldn't be the first time we all got together to watch TV."

Nancy, Rita, and Sharon arrive and fill the living room with their laughter and complaints. A few minutes later, the bell rings again.

"Hi!" Dot says.

"What, no catch phrase?" I  ask.

"That was *so* last year," she laughs.

I can honestly say I'm not sorry to see it go.

Billy arrives not long after.

"Sorry I'm late. I'm swamped with homework. My mom's taking her job as teacher way too seriously," Billy says. "I can't wait to go back to school with you guys."

The doorbell rings one more time and I'm happy to see Hank standing on the doorstep.

"Thanks for the invite!" he says.

"My pleasure," I say - and really mean it.

My friends and I join Mom and her friends in the TV room and relax for the first time in weeks. One thing's for sure: there's nothing like being able to live your reality in private.

# #LeaveUsAReview

Please support us by leaving a review. The more reviews we get, the more books we will write.

# #FollowUsOnInstagram

@AnnieEmoji * @KevinEmoji

# #BooksInTheSeries

## Horse Party * Emoji Olympics
## Call of Doodie * Reality TV

#MakeaCameo

Want to be a Character in the next
Emoji Adventures Book? Enter at:
www.EmojiAdventuresBook.com

MONTAGE PUBLISHING

www.MontagePublishing.com

Made in the USA
San Bernardino, CA
10 October 2016